DANCING ON THE SAND
A Story of an Atlantic Blue Crab

SMITHSONIAN OCEANIC COLLECTION

To Lynell, who opened the door—K.H.

To Dahweed, see you in moons, man—J.P.

Book copyright © 1999 Trudy Corporation and the Smithsonian Institution, Washington, DC 20560.

Published by Soundprints, an imprint of Trudy Corporation, Norwalk, Connecticut.
www.soundprints.com

Book layout: Scott Findlay
Editor: Judy Gitenstein

First Paperback Edition 1999
10 9 8 7 6 5 4 3
Printed in China

Acknowledgments:
    Our very special thanks to Dr. Raymond B. Manning of the Department of Invertebrate Zoology at the Smithsonian Institution's National Museum of Natural History for his curatorial review.

ISBN: 978-1-59249-194-0 (pbk.)

The Library of Congress Cataloging-in-Publication Data below applies only to the hardcover edition of this book.

Library of Congress Cataloging-in-Publication Data

Hollenbeck, Kathleen M.

  Dancing on the sand: a story of an Atlantic blue crab / written by Kathleen Hollenbeck;
  illustrated by Joanie Popeo—1st ed.
       p.   cm.
  Summary: Blue Crab scuttles through the shallow waters of the Chesapeake Bay to find a mate, to molt, and to avoid predators while waiting for her eggs to hatch.
       ISBN: 1-56899-730-2
  1. Blue crabs—Juvenile Fiction. [1. Blue Crabs—Fiction. 2. Crabs—Fiction. 3. Chesapeake Bay (Md. and Va.—Fiction.]
  1. Popeo, Joanie, ill. II. Title.
  PZ10.3.H716Dan 1999   98-42566
  [E]—dc21   CIP
                                                                        AC

DANCING ON THE SAND

A Story of an Atlantic Blue Crab

by Kathleen M. Hollenbeck   Illustrated by Joanie Popeo

Soundprints®
Where Children Discover...

It is a bright morning in late August. Sunlight sparkles on the Chesapeake Bay. Gentle waves lap the Maryland shore, leaving a trail of white foam along the water's edge.

Beneath the shallow water, Blue Crab scuttles sideways on the sand. Perched on slender stalks atop her shell, tiny black eyes allow her to see on all sides. She uses her four antennae to help her to find food and to sense danger.

Blue Crab is hungry and begins her search for food. A plump killifish swims into view. Alert, Blue Crab stands very still. The killifish darts closer. Instantly, Blue Crab lunges, seizes the fish with a powerful claw, and eats it.

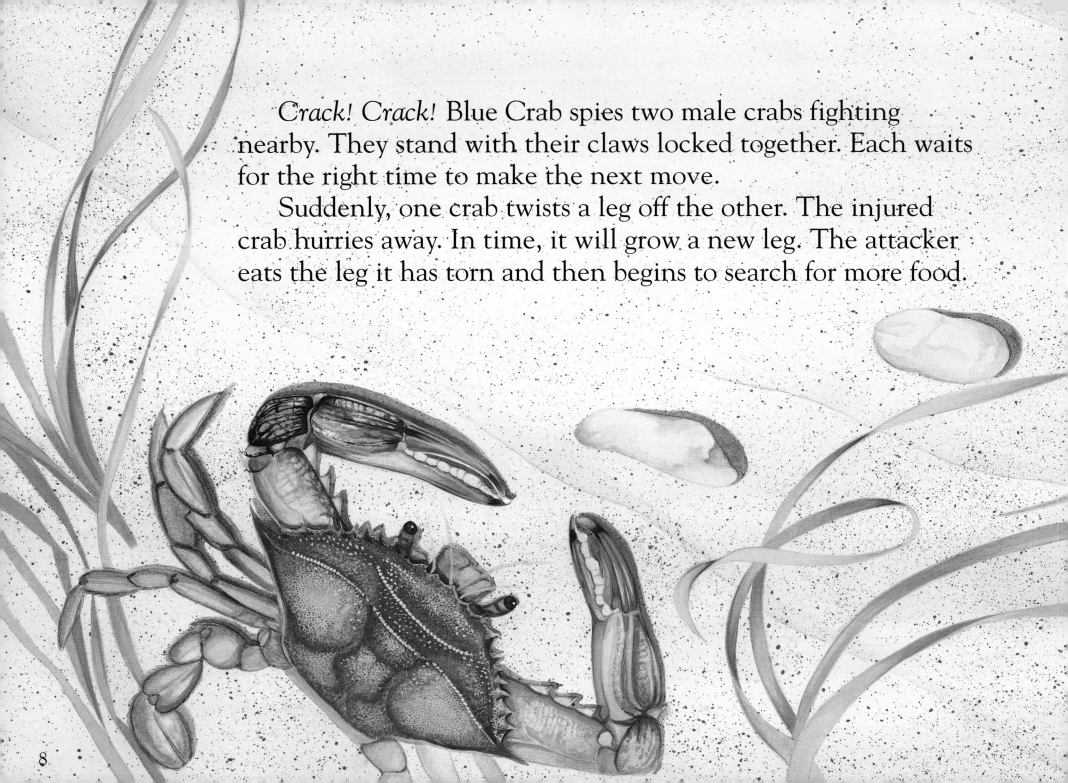

Crack! Crack! Blue Crab spies two male crabs fighting nearby. They stand with their claws locked together. Each waits for the right time to make the next move.

Suddenly, one crab twists a leg off the other. The injured crab hurries away. In time, it will grow a new leg. The attacker eats the leg it has torn and then begins to search for more food.

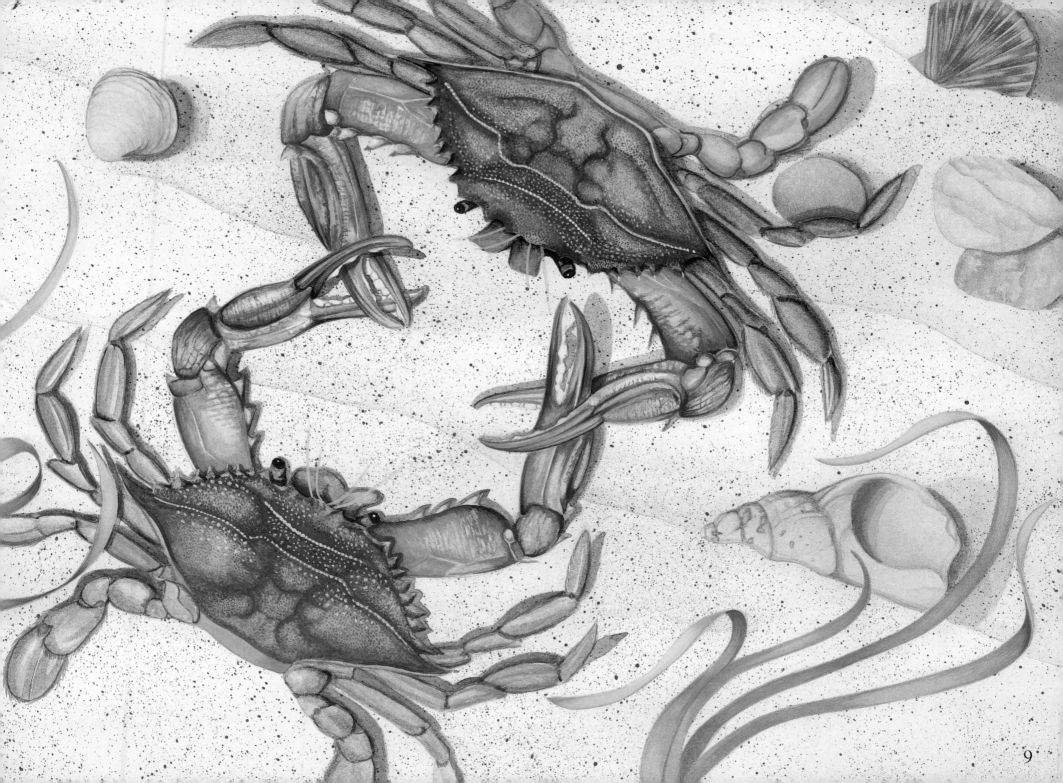

Blue Crab senses other movement. She turns to see a male blue crab standing high on his three pairs of walking legs. Aware that she is watching, the male stretches his claws straight out on each side and lifts his hind pair of legs up behind him. These legs are shaped like paddles and he waves them quickly from side to side. He is dancing for Blue Crab, showing that he wants to be her mate.

Blue Crab needs a mate, for the time is near when she will molt. She will cast off her old shell and grow a bigger one. She has molted many times before, but this molt is special. This time Blue Crab will become an adult, able to make eggs. During the molting, she will need a male crab to protect her and to mate with her.

The male crab snaps his body backward and kicks up sand. Joining the dance, Blue Crab waves her claws quickly from side to side and scuttles closer.

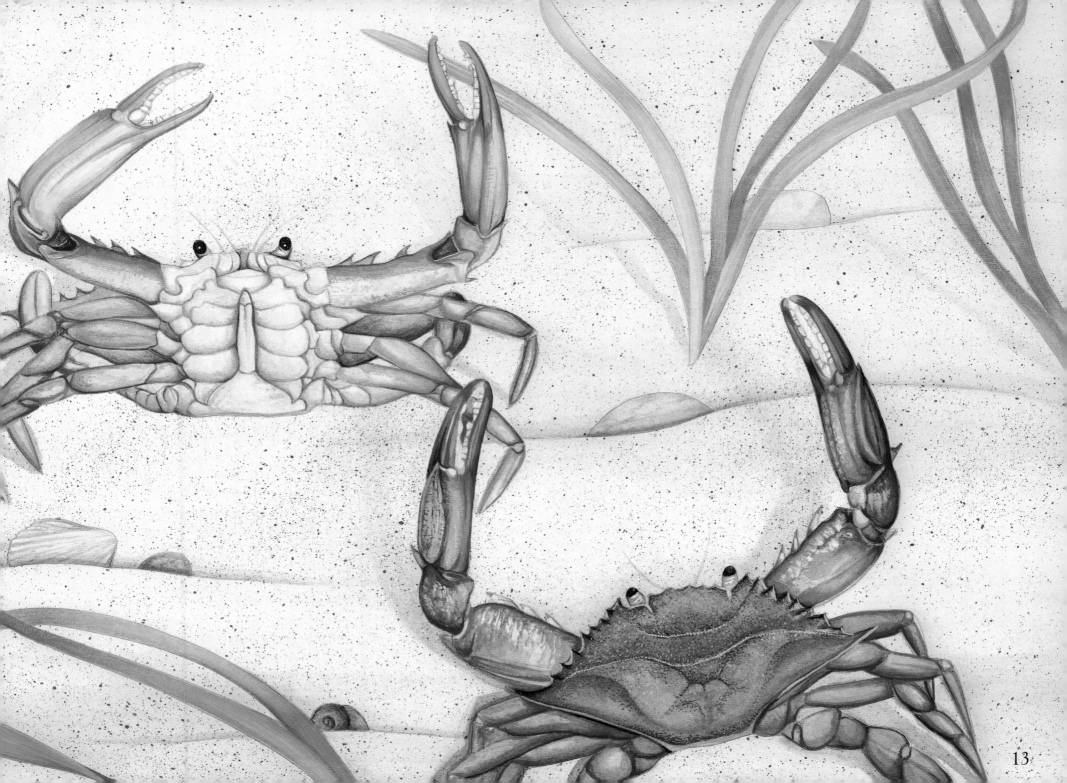

Directly in front of the male crab, Blue Crab turns around and moves backward bit by bit until she is underneath him. She folds in her claws and allows herself to be carried.

Wrapping his six walking legs around her, the male crab swims with his paddles. He searches for a hiding place where Blue Crab can molt.

Blue Crab's mate settles in a hollow spot next to a large clump of eel grass. He stands high, making a protective cage around Blue Crab with his legs. Blue Crab's shell splits. The time has come for her to molt.

Blue Crab moves apart from her mate. For the next few hours, she works with all her might. Little by little she pulls her soft body out of the old hard shell.

With the male crab standing guard, Blue Crab rests and takes in water to enlarge her new shell. The shell is paper-soft and will take several days to harden. During this time, the male crab mates with Blue Crab so she will be able to make eggs in the spring. Then he carries her as before, keeping her safe while her soft shell grows hard and strong.

In early September, Blue Crab leaves her mate and begins to move south. Her eggs will need the warmer and saltier water found there.

Sometimes she walks, stretching and bending her legs to hurry sideways on the sand. Sometimes she uses her paddles to swim. When Blue Crab rests, she protects herself by hiding among seaweed or burying herself in the mud.

Close to shore one day, Blue Crab senses danger. A pair of long, thin legs stretches up out of the water from the sea bottom. They belong to a great blue heron. The heron stretches its neck toward Blue Crab and pierces the water with its long, spear-like beak. Blue Crab jumps back and burrows into the mud. She stays there until the heron is gone.

As Blue Crab makes her way along the sand, a striped bass looms near. When she was young, Blue Crab would hide to escape such a fish. Now strong and fast, Blue Crab swims away from it.

The bay grows cold. Blue Crab buries herself in the mud and remains there through the winter.

When spring arrives, Blue Crab reaches the mouth of the Chesapeake Bay. She has completed her journey. Here in the salty waters, Blue Crab spawns about two million tiny eggs. They cling in clusters to her abdomen, or apron.

While her eggs develop, Blue Crab hunts for food. One afternoon, she seizes something tasty with her claw. It tugs back and drags Blue Crab up out of the water. Blue Crab has been caught! She hangs from a piece of bait at the end of a string. Her eggs glisten in the sunlight.

The string jerks sharply. Blue Crab lets go of the bait and falls into a pail held by human hands. Suddenly, the pail overturns, sending Blue Crab plunging back into the water. She lands on the bottom, then scuttles quickly away, leaving a muddy cloud behind her.

Blue Crab cannot know that because she is carrying eggs, the crabber set her free.

Several weeks later, Blue Crab's eggs hatch in the warm, salty ocean. They drift off, teeny tiny creatures floating through the water. Some will be eaten by small fish. Others will continue to molt and grow into blue crabs like their parents.

On her own again, Blue Crab will spend her days traveling along tidal creeks and rivers until she returns to the sparkling waters of the Chesapeake Bay.

About the Atlantic Blue Crab

The Atlantic blue crab lives in shallow waters along the Atlantic coast, from New England to the northern shores of South America. Legend has it that the animal was originally called "blue claw crab" because of the large blue claws found on the male crab. Females have claws tipped with bright red and orange.

Blue crabs have five pairs of legs that extend from the side of the body: one pair in front, near its eyes; three pairs in the midsection used for walking; and one pair in the rear used for swimming.

The female crab molts—or sheds her shell—approximately twenty-seven times before reaching the adult stage. Just before the molt that will make her an adult, she emits a chemical to attract a mature male crab. This male remains with her throughout the molting process to protect her from predators and to ensure that no other male comes near. After molting, the female crab mates with the male, while her shell is soft.

In spring and sometimes again in the fall, the female crab produces approximately 2 million eggs, which cling to her abdomen in clusters. Crabbers who catch such a crab release her so as not to destroy the eggs.

Only a tiny number of a blue crab's eggs make it to adulthood. Many will die because of improper conditions. For example, the water may not have enough oxygen; it may be too warm or too cold; it may be too salty or not salty enough. In addition, the eggs may be attacked by fungus or by predators. Those eggs that live molt often, changing from microscopic larvae into pinhead-sized crabs within two months.

The scientific name for blue crab is *Callinectes sapidus*. *Callinectes* means "beautiful swimmer" in Greek; *sapidus* means "tasty" in Latin.

Glossary

apron: A female crab's abdomen.

molt: To cast off an old shell or covering so a new one can grow in its place.

spawn: To produce a large number of eggs.

Points of Interest in this Book